PRINCESS PENELOPE

by Todd Mack   illustrated by Julia Gran

SCHOLASTIC INC.

New York Toronto London Auckland Sydney
Mexico City New Delhi Hong Kong Buenos Aires

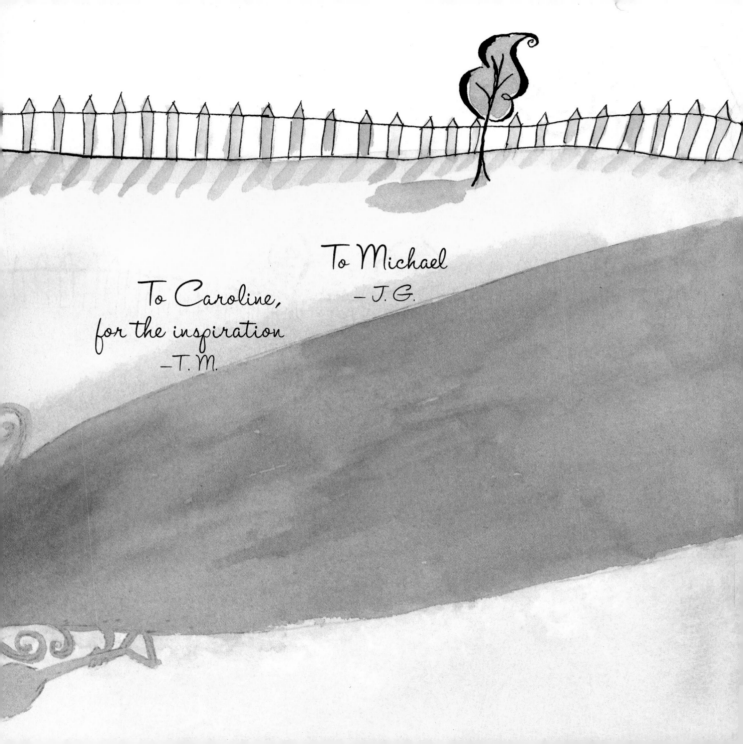

To Caroline,
for the inspiration
–T. M.

To Michael
– J. G.

PENELOPE was a princess.
She was absolutely certain.

She read lots of fairy tales,
so she was an
EXPERT on princesses.

Her grandmother even gave her a princess crown.
"This is just like the crown I used to wear when
I was a girl," she told Penelope.

Every morning, Penelope was awoken
by a kiss from the king and the queen.
"GOOD MORNING, MY
LITTLE PRINCESS!"
the queen always
reveled.

"I'M PENELOPE,
AND I AM A PRINCESS!"
she sang at the top of her lungs.
The king and the queen
had to share a room and a bed,
but Penelope had her very own bed
in her very own room,
JUST LIKE A PRINCESS.

Princesses had chambermaids
who buttoned and zipped them.
So did Penelope.

Princesses changed their outfits
many times a day.
Penelope LOVED to change
her outfits.

"I'M PENELOPE,
AND I AM A
PRINCESS!"
she cheered
as she pranced
through the palace.

Princesses sat
on thrones.
Penelope had
LOTS
of thrones.

"I'M PENELOPE, AND I AM A PRINCESS,"
she announced at her midday meal.

Princesses ate FANCY foods,
served on SPECIAL dishes.
They had servants who waited on them
hand and foot. So did Penelope.

The servants cleaned up after their princess and comforted her in times of need.

"I'M PENELOPE, AND I AM A PRINCESS,"
she caroled when she strolled through her kingdom.
Princesses rode in chariots. Penelope had LOTS of chariots.
Princesses were famous. Penelope was famous.

Everywhere she went, people stopped and waved.
They smiled and threw kisses.
Many of them she'd never met before.
They ALL told her she was beautiful.

Princesses made rules.

PENELOPE made rules.

The king said she ruled the roost.

Princesses liked to give commands and make demands.

PENELOPE liked to give commands and make demands.

Sometimes she had to sit on one of her thrones
after making too many demands.

"I'M PENELOPE, AND I AM A PRINCESS,"
she chanted while the queen drew her bath.
Every night, Penelope was pampered, just like a princess.

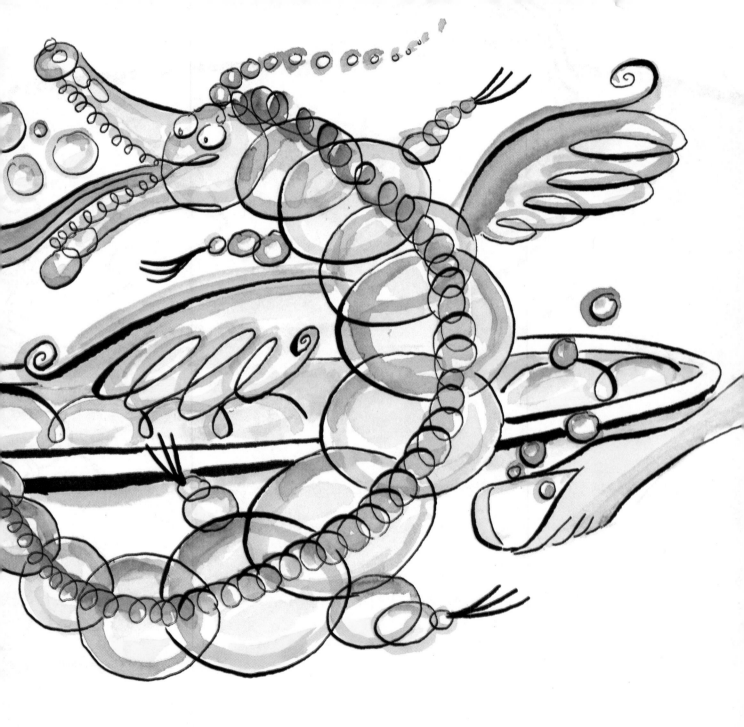

Then she put on a royal robe and climbed into bed.
The king read her favorite fairy tale before he
and the queen kissed Penelope good night.
"SWEET DREAMS, MY LITTLE PRINCESS,"
the king always whispered.

Penelope was a princess.
She was absolutely certain.